ELIZABETH MUELLER

Novels by Elizabeth Mueller

Darkspell, YA Paranormal Romance

Short Stories

Avenger's Angel, All Made of Hinges: A Mormon Steampunk
Anthology, Book 1, Anthology

The Cog Prince, Masquerade: Oddly Suited, Anthology

Non-fiction

The Insecure Writer's Support Group Guide to Publishing and Beyond,
(a multiple author project)

ELIZABETH MUELLER

ISBN: 9781711870359

Edited by Cornerstone Press
Cover Design by Cornerstone Press
Art by jimo663 on Pixabay.com

10 9 8 7 6 5 4 3 2 1

Dedicated to Cheyanna, Levi, Autumn, Dallas, and Weston — remember inhibitions cramp true happiness. Love you!

Chapter One

boots and jeans

I knew which was worse than competing against Yana for the leading role of The Nutcracker and it was going back to Texas. Sure, I had found it exciting when Dad declared missing big city life just as much as Mom preferred to sleep on haybales at night. It was good when they first split up but got old pretty fast with all the back-and-forthing. That part totally bummed my schedules.

Don't get me wrong. I love Dad. I love Mom. I just don't like the silly business of *whose turn it is*. I couldn't wait until I was eighteen. One more year…

"Cora, did you hear me?"

I saw Julie's mouth twist out the corner of my eye. If I let my guard down, she'd make my life harder. "Of course I heard you," I said, laughing at the unsightly image of Yana midsneeze. "I love you, Tiana." I kissed my phone and flicked onto the next photo. Tiana, my best friend, loved photography

1

more than ballet, and she was pretty good at capturing prized moments.

"Cora." Julie she snatched my phone. "You're way too distracted. That's your problem."

I closed my eyes and drew in a deep breath, counting to ten. I didn't need another person telling me what to do. I didn't have the best temperament, either. I suppose it ran through Dad's veins, hence, the savage ripping apart of a twenty-year marriage. My eyes popped open and I gave Julie a wide smile; far be it for me to allow her to step all over me.

I said with a sarcastically sweet tone, "That's not what Madame Beaulieu says." I tore my phone back from her. "I'm very promising."

"Not with this thing around." She took the phone back and stuffed it down her fathomless purse. With a triumphant laugh, she raised her nose into the air and crossed her leg as our cab slowed at an intersection. *"Now* your chances have increased."

"Ugh." I folded my arms and stared unseeingly out the snow-splattered window. I refused to think of the reason why I had to visit Mom. Irritation crept up my back as I thought of the losses I had to face by obliging her. "Don't you think this is dumb? Doesn't Mom know what I'm up against? We're talking about my abandoning the ballet." I slammed my head against the headrest. "I mean, why now?"

"Cora!" Julie gasped. "She backed down when Dad told her you needed to focus on ballet a few years back. The least you could do is go willingly."

"Oh, please, Julie." I swung my gaze to her with a harsh glare. "It's all good for you. You don't have to take time off work to indulge her whims."

Julie swore, slapping her knee. "Have you forgotten why she needs you? This is not about you, Cora, and you know it."

"I'd prefer not to think of it at all. It's about what they want. Always has been. Whose side are you on anyway? Have *you* forgotten how hard going back-and-forth was on your life?" I thinned my lips, sinking into the cushions with a heaving sigh. My heart fell at the thought of leaving the ways of fast city life for the slow laze of the ranch. Mom needed me, but I was too angry to think of the nitty-gritty. "Easy for you to say as you're not the one going. I'm giving up The Nutcracker so give me my phone so that I can say goodbye to Tiana."

"I thought you already have?" she spoke with a soft voice. She handed my phone back, her gold rings flashing.

"In person, yes." I bit my lip, my finger hesitating above the tiny keyboard. I glanced at Julie's hand as she patted my knee.

"I know this is difficult for you," she whispered. "And I've had my fair share of imposition, but you need to remember that Mom and Dad love you, and sometimes they need us in places even if it's a huge sacrifice for us."

I tilted my head back and gave my best pouty face and snapped a selfie. "You only had to sacrifice a year of inconvenience—and I, four."

She sighed. "I'm here for you, Cora."

I shook my head and typed my farewell to Tiana. *I'm at the airport now. If you remember, no service where I'm going.* I attached my selfie. *I'll see you whenever? BTW, I love the pic of Yana's sneeze. Try to send more!*

Everything from there passed with a blur. I barely remember my sister's hug and boarding the jet. I barely remember the gut-wrenching feeling of take-off and the releasing seatbelt announcement. I barely remember the long hours of travel and landing in the San Antonio airport. Everything whirled and buzzed and tossed me about until I finally found myself locked in Mom's arms.

"Oh, baby girl, here you are. Here you are!" Her big blue eyes with dark brown eyelashes spikey with tears took me in. She sniffled and wiped her nose with the back of her hand. "Tell me, how have you been?" She angled me and led me from the thick crowds.

I looked down at her scuffed boots and Wrangler jeans. My heart, for a quick second, gave a kick. Something about her outfit made my stomach both flutter and fall. Fall because it reminded me of what I had been missing, flutter because there was something my heart missed before the falling out.

Chapter Two

horsehair and brats

M om tried to get me to warm up to her by bringing my favorite treat: good old-fashioned oatmeal and raisin cookies. But I couldn't stomach them this time. I folded my arms, my knees to my chest as we drove through the long stretch of the lonely highway.

"Cora," she said, her voice cutting off right after saying my name as if she hesitated to say more. "I am so very sorry you lost your part with The Nutcracker. It means a lot to me that you come last minute."

I closed my eyes and dropped my head back, pushing away the thought of Yana's smug face the day Dad walked in and signed me out. I jerked my head toward the dark window, unable to reply. I cringed at my reflection when I saw just how frizzy my perfect hair became from the stifling humidity.

"Dan and I will stay out of your way. You can have Julie's old room."

Dan. He was the guy who stole Mom's heart a year and a half after the divorce.

"What about Jesse? I bet he misses you," she said with a singsong tune.

"Jesse?" I spun in place to look at her, remembering the fat little boy who used to chase me around with earthworm-filled mudballs. "As in, Roly-Poly Jesse?" Okay. He wasn't exactly little being that he was about three years older.

She burst out laughing, wrenching my heart with its nostalgic familiarity. "The very one."

"I thought he left for college the day you remarried?" I faced forward at the glaring headlights of the oncoming traffic. Even then, I still had not seen him. He had stopped coming by long before, and I was too angry to care for his reasons. "I doubt it," I finally answered as I lifted my leg and rotated my ankle.

Mom shot me a secretive smile. She grunted, her hand clutching her rounded belly.

"Are you alright?" I asked, glancing down at her stomach.

"Yeah. Just the baby. He keeps me awake at all times of the day and night."

That was the very reason I was needed. Dan and she were planning on going to Houston to have the baby, and I was to look after my half-brother. Didn't they have neighbors who could do that? I pulled a thick lock of hair from my bun and frowned. One of the biggest reasons I didn't like Texas was how the humidity killed the sleek smoothness of my hair. I threw it behind me with a growl.

She reached across the bench seat and squeezed my knee. "Thank you for coming down so last-minute. Julie couldn't make it because of her work and there was no one else."

I huffed. "Yeah."

"What about Acorn?" She sucked in her lips and made a left-hand turn.

"Acorn?" I was confused by the sudden change of topic.

"Have you forgotten about Acorn?" She sent me a brief glance of surprise.

"Acorn?" I said again but with a surprised squeak, momentarily forgetting

New York. How could I have forgotten? "You still have her?"

"Of course, we do, sweet pea." She glimpsed at me with a tender smile.

"B-but I thought you—I thought Dan… What?" This time, I turned a full ninety-degree to face her. Acorn was my horse from when I was a little girl. It had broken my heart the day Mom said they couldn't keep her. "I thought you sold her?"

Mom blinked as we turned off the highway onto a dark and lonely road. "It turns out that I refused to sell Acorn no matter how much Dan pushed." Her voice was so soft, I wasn't sure I heard right.

"Why would he decide to keep her?" I asked as my mind reverted to ballet.

She gave me a meaningful look before returning her eyes to the stretch of road. "Because she needs you."

"You know, a horse can't replace ballet," I grumbled. "I doubt anything will make me happy." I shoved the cookies aside. She needed to know just how annoyed I felt about all this. But the closer we got to the ranch, the more I couldn't stop thinking of Acorn's warm coat and thick hair. I guessed I did miss her after all, but Mom didn't need to know that. We finally turned onto the dirt road.

The sound of Mom's door shutting pulled me from my thoughts. Have we stopped?

I stepped from the truck, my hands in my pockets. The stables weren't that far. A horse neighed from the brightly lit building in the near distance. I started for them but turned to look at Mom. When she wasn't watching, I broke out into a hard run across the tall grass.

"Acorn!" I shouted, my heart thumping as fast as my feet. "Acorn!" I slammed the door open and ran straight into a body whose arms caught me with a deep voice that made me scream and jump back. Pushing my hair from my eyes, I gazed at a very sculpted face of a young man with laughing brown eyes.

"Excuse me," I said as I shrugged his hands off me, irritated with the obstruction yet painfully conscious of my frizzy hair and clingy clothes. Curse Texas humidity! His watchful eyes didn't leave mine, but I craned my neck to look behind him. "Wait a minute, who are you?"

He placed his gloved hands to his chest clad with a white T-shirt beneath a plaid button-down. "Cora Lynne, former horse extraordinaire-turned-ballerina does not know who I am?"

This time, I surveyed him with my arms crossed. He wore boots and jeans that hugged muscular thighs. The shirt fit him just as finely. By this time, he had removed his Stetson hat, causing a lock of dark brown hair to fall across his knowing, familiar gaze.

No way...

"Jesse?" I blurted, taking a step back. I shook my head.

"At your service." He gave a little bow.

"But how?" I moved past him and gazed into each stall in search of Acorn.

His laughter was deep, unfamiliar, and nerve-tingling. "But how what?"

"I mean, how is it you're here? Aren't you supposed to be off at college?" I didn't turn to look at him. Four horses so far but no Acorn.

"Aren't you supposed to be marching beneath an overgrown Christmas tree?" he countered.

I stopped and turned to him, the twinkle in his eyes made my toes tingle. I wiggled them and tore my gaze from him to a nearby stall. "Where's Acorn?"

"Exercising," he said as he returned his hat to his head.

"Where?" I looked past him to the open door. I didn't wait for his answer but went around him to the corral where I found her prancing about. Brilliant lights glinted off my eyelashes, and I shadowed my hand above my eyes.

"She sure is a beauty." Jesse's velvety voice made me jump.

I moved from him as he had stood too close to me. "I know." I made myself not look at this stranger, whoever he was. Though I recognized the soft twinkling brown of his eyes, it was not his face or body or voice. How could it be? Had time changed him so much? Before I could do something that would betray my thoughts, I slipped through the fence and ran up to Acorn.

"Cora, wait!" he shouted.

"Acorn!" I cried out, my heart bursting with joy. Acorn turned her head to me and did what I never expected her to do: she lifted her body high into the air, her hooves flashing right in front of me. I dropped to the dirt and covered my head. Instead of feeling the sharp punishment of her hooves dashing me to bits, I felt Jesse's strong presence beside me.

"Hey, calm there, girl. That's right."

I looked up at him and jumped back up with a glower. "What did you do to her?"

"Me?" He chuckled, holding the halter. Acorn tossed her head and took a sidestep. "She startles easily. It was you."

"Never." I breathed. "She loves me."

"It has been three years."

"No, it has not." I lifted my chin and scowled. He arched a thick brow with a tilt of his head, his lips forming a word that I didn't let him say. "Jesse is such a liar, Acorn. How can so much time go?" I touched her soft nose as she snuffled my hand. Still agitated with his declaration, I said, "Don't you have a classroom to be in or something?"

"My, my, Cora Lynne, you sure are feistier than I remember."

"And you, Jesse, are not who you're supposed to be." As soon as those words were out, my face flushed hot.

He chuckled as he led my horse into the stables. "And who am I supposed to be?"

Short and fat, I was about to say but remembered myself. I followed him. "Never mind. Where are you taking Acorn?" I glided beside Jesse, upset at how he easily commanded my horse who didn't seem to know me.

"Back to her stall. She needs to turn in for the night." He gazed over his shoulder and gave me a flirtatious wink.

My mouth dropped open, and I lost my step and fell behind the fast-limbed pace of both man and beast. After gathering my wit, I caught up with them. "Cora."

"What?"

"My name is Cora. I don't use Lynne anymore."

"Cora now, is it?"

I stiffened. Was everything a joke to him? "Are you making fun of me?"

He entered the stables and didn't close the door until I entered. "I hardly know you anymore."

"But you have this smile and laughter about you." I pointed to his face, angry at how he made light of me.

"It's called a sense of humor. Surely New York has—oh never mind." He pulled a wide brush from the top of a shelf and with deft movements, swept Acorn's coat.

"Here, let me do that." I bumped Jesse aside with my hip and snatched the thing from him. As my fingers grazed his, a sharp tingle made me gasp. I turned to him to see if he noticed, but he gazed down at the toe of his boot. "Fine." I lowered my hand and said, "I apologize for being such a brat. I'm not sure how to act around you anymore."

"Why?" His lashes flickered as he gazed at me from beneath the brim of his hat.

My heart leapt. "Well, uh, I-I." I bit my lip and brushed Acorn's brown coat with the same movements he used.

"Why, I do believe Cora is speechless."

The laughter in his voice irked me. "You!" I turned on him and flicked the bristles so that the air between us filled with tiny, short hairs. He choked and coughed on them which, in turn, made me laugh. Soon, we both coughed on the drifting hairs.

"Whatever I am doing wrong, and if this is you being a brat, I sure won't stop now," Jesse said.

Chapter Three

toddlers and good-byes

I stretched across Julie's old king-sized bed. It felt delicious to extend my cramped muscles after the long and tedious trip. Then there was the run-in with Jesse. My hand still tingled from our accidental touch. I thought of his mouth and how his lips might feel pressed up against mine. The tingle in my hand made me shiver. A knock startled me from my thoughts and I gasped.

"Come in," I called out, rubbing my eyes in case the visitor might notice my fantasizing.

"Here, I brought you supper. I thought you might be starving after such a long trip." Mom came in.

I sat up and shook my hair from my shoulders, a thought occurring to me. "Wait a minute," I said, narrowing my eyes at her when she handed me the steaming plate. "You knew Jesse would be here, didn't you?"

She lowered onto the bed with a small shrug. "Yeah, I did. Isn't he a dreamboat?"

"Dreamboat? Mom, dreamboat?" I threw myself back, but she caught the plate before it splattered to the floor.

"I can see he did not disappoint," she said in a purring voice.

"Ugh." I sprang back up. "I made a total dork of myself. He's so different."

"You mean you didn't recognize those dark and charming eyes? That dimple?"

"Mom!" I glared at her, irritated. I thought back on how I'd crashed into him. For a person who took pride in her sure-footedness, I was such a bumbling fool. I glanced down at the plate in her hand. "I don't eat potatoes, but the roast beef and broccoli sure look tasty."

"Before you know it, Dan will have you eating his famous chili poppers." She smiled.

"Chili poppers?" I laughed with a shake of my head. Had I forgotten so much?

"You'll see," she said as she set the plate on the edge of the bed. "Erik is asleep now, but you'll get to meet him come morning."

"Erik," I repeated. My little two-year-old half-brother. I'd only seen him as a pudgy-faced little man from the many photos Mom would send.

"By the way, you have a better chance at pretending to choke on your food than rubbing your eyes if you don't want me to see you thinking of Jesse," Mom said with a secretive smile before slipping away.

"What? No!" I leaped from the bed and shut the door and leaned against it, covering my face. How did she know? I hadn't been around long enough.

"The dreamy eyes gave you away, Cora," she said through the door.

"Dimple? Really?" I shot back. My face warmed and the image of his lips came to view. A sudden question popped into my head and I yanked the door open. "What's he doing here, anyway?" But I was too late. Mom had already left.

Too tired to chase after her, I finished supper and crawled into bed. *Pliés* and *manages* and *chaîné* turns filled my dreams. Yana's jeering expression melted into Jesse's sultry one. Just as I was about to dive into that kiss, strong hands shook me awake.

"Cora, time to get up," Mom said.

"What?" I said with a raspy croak.

She rocked a clinging Erik at her hip. "Dan made breakfast and we'll be out for most of the day."

"We?" I groaned, dropping back down.

"Today is training for you with Erik. Dan will explain what all needs to be done outside. Come on." She nudged my feet with her knee.

"You never told me what Jesse's doing here." I sat up with a yawn.

"He's our help." Mom was already walking out my door so I couldn't see her face.

"Help? Then what do you need me for?" I scooted from the bed and stretched my legs.

"Erik needs you."

"And you couldn't find anyone else to watch him." I glared at her retreating back.

"And it never hurts to play matchmaker."

"Matchmaker—what? Mom!" I ran after her. Erik giggled as he reached out to me. We moved down the staircase that swept into the grand living room where a towering, unlit Christmas tree loomed. Wrapped presents were tucked into the corner beside it. Garland decorated the banisters and hearth above five stockings. Arranged upon the mantle was a hand-carved Nativity set. The spacious, open kitchen yawned straight ahead. I paused. Not how I remembered this place.

"Good morning!" Dan boomed in his *Kiss Me, I Cook* apron. He set a big plate of bacon at the center of the kitchen table. "Careful, it's piping hot."

"Oooh, I came just in time." I sat in the nearest chair and gazed around me. Pancakes. Biscuits. Orange juice. Sausage. "What's the occasion, or do you eat restaurant-style every morning?"

Mom laughed and Dan grinned. "You are the occasion," he said, spinning back to the stove.

Erik twisted in his highchair after Mom buckled him in.

"Me?"

"Yep." Dan whipped off his apron and joined Mom at the table with a kiss.

I had to ignore the uncomfortable squirming that went on in my stomach every time I thought of her with someone other than Dad, but then again, Dad had moved on as well. I sighed.

"You are saving us from having to find some stranger to watch Erik," Mom explained after seeing my confusion.

"Acorn missed you something terrible," Dan said.

I laughed. "She doesn't know me anymore."

"Point proven."

Just then, the side door opened and in stepped Jesse. He removed his cowboy hat and whooped. "Looks like I arrived in the nick of time." His gaze found me and my eyes found his lips. Just as I remembered them in my dreams. Fierce heat pressed against my ears and I looked at Mom who wiggled her eyebrows. "Looks like a chair was saved and everything, too," he said. He pulled the chair out from right next to me and I froze.

Why didn't I notice that before? I frowned at Mom. At least this time she had the decency to look away.

After the blessing was said, we passed the platters around and picked as much as we liked. I veered away from the carbs but piled on the bacon. I dared a flakey biscuit that melted in my mouth and I chugged down a healthy portion of orange juice.

"Wow, Cora," Jesse said. "I didn't know that ballerinas ate so much."

Feeling incredulous, I stabbed him with a look. "Unlike you, Jesse, we ballerinas use a whole lot more calories to maintain our stamina and form." He laughed, held his hands up and scooted back when he was done. I flinched when his sleeve brushed my bare arm. It didn't hurt. I was so keenly aware of his proximity, it made me dizzy.

"May I be excused?" Jesse asked.

"Of course," Mom said, motioning him away with her fork.

"Thank you." He stood with a few dishes in hand.

"I have a better idea." Dan first addressed me and then turned to the intruder. "Jesse, I'd like for you to show Cora around the ranch. With her stamina and form, we can sure use that here."

I huffed.

"Sounds like fun. I'll be out with the horses." Jesse winked at me as he walked backward. When he reached the door, he backed out and closed it. Through the curtained window, I watched him return the hat to his head and leave.

"I think someone's goose is cooked," Dan said, rising from his chair with several empty plates.

I ignored his strange remark. "What about Erik?" I rose.

"He goes down for a regular nap at one. He sleeps until about two, two-thirty, sometimes three depending on how much he plays—"

"That's a hint," Dan interrupted.

I glared at him.

"—his bedtime is at eight and he sleeps like a rock, also depending on how busy you keep him."

"That's another hint," Dan said.

I rolled my eyes. "I don't know how to keep a toddler busy." I looked from Dan to Mom.

"Well, let's see: He knows how to toss the chicken feed, the horse feed, he knows how to gather acorns." Mom smiled with a satisfied nod.

"And he's a real fast runner," Dan interjected with a pointed finger.

Mom burst out laughing. She unbuckled Erik, who raised his hands with sharp laughter.

"Chicknas!" he cried out.

"He loves chasing them chickens." Mom's eyes shined. "Don't you?"

"Okay. I'll keep that in mind." Shouldn't be that hard, right?

"Make sure you wash his hands after each outdoor adventure, and his bath is at seven forty-five before his bed. It helps to calm him."

"Sounds easy enough."

Dan and Mom exchanged looks.

"What?"

"We've been told that he's a super handful, and, well, with your stamina and form, you'll be up to standard." Mom laughed.

"Ugh!" I dropped my head against my shoulders. "I shouldn't have said anything."

"At least you won't get out of shape." Dan scrubbed the dishes down and loaded the dishwasher.

"Then there's riding the horses. You can do that after Erik is in bed." Mom cleaned Erik's hands and face with a dish towel from the drawer while he wiggled.

My stomach sank at the prospect of my day being filled with so much activity. Well, I was used to activity back at home. Always busy with school. Assignments. Ballet. Practicing at home. Friends. I guess it wasn't so bad. "How will I know if Erik needs me while I'm out and about?"

"Thank goodness for baby monitors!" Mom pointed to a radio looking thing that sat on the counter.

"Does the range go that far?" I asked. I walked into the kitchen and helped put away the leftovers.

"It's the best out there," Dan said, shutting the dishwasher with a satisfying click.

Mom set Erik down and he sprang forward to the living room where his foam blocks were scattered. "Thank you so much for everything, sweetie." She leaned in and placed a kiss on my cheek.

"We'll see you later this evening." Dan grabbed a set of keys from the top of the fridge. "Danielle, er, your mom and I are going into town for some last-minute shopping. It won't take long."

"I hope that's okay." She patted my cheek. Before I could object, she said, "Bye, Erik sweetling!" She blew him a kiss and waved at me. Dan opened the same door Jesse had left through, and out they both swept. "Call if you need anything," she said to me as the door closed.

"What? Now? Mom!" I started for them, but Erik's responding farewell stopped me. I turned and looked at him, suddenly feeling vulnerable. So many what-ifs hit me at once that I forgot how to breathe. Scooping him up, I did the first thing that came to mind: I ran out the door in search of Jesse.

Chapter Four

apples and dinosaurs

gain, the day hit me with such a force of humidity that I mourned my hair. I made my way to the horses with Erik, who squirmed so much I had to set him down. Big mistake! He darted away and vanished around the corner before I could blink.

"Erik!" I started forward. "Erik, come back here right now!" Did Mom say anything about a reward system? Dad sure had that down to a tee. Come to think of it, Mom wasn't near as organized as he. I grunted, unable to find the little guy. Panic squeezed my heart. "Erik, where are you?"

"Hey." Jesse's deep voice jolted me and I screamed, my fist coming around and smacking him square in the chest. He took a step back, his eyes wide, but his mouth lifted to one side. "You have yourself quite the hit!"

"Don't mess with me," I muttered as a joke, but it sounded more like a threat. "I can't find Erik."

"Did you check the chickens?"

Just then, the chickens squawked and squabbled up a storm. Last I remembered, the chicken coop was located on the south side beside the pear orchard, but instead, it was now a pigpen. My heart sank. "Where are the chickens?"

"Next to the horses." Jesse moved his shoulders as a way of invitation to follow him. "I'll show ya."

"Thank you." I sounded defensive. Not bothering to apologize, I trudged forward. He didn't move until I was beside him. I made a face. I preferred to follow him so that he wouldn't look at me. It also gave me a chance to look at him all I wanted without inhibition.

"You're pretty when you blush."

"Are you saying I'm not pretty when I don't?"

His eyebrow arched. "No. You are pretty now. Cora, we're not really strangers. Sure, a lot of time has passed, but we grew up together. Why are you treating me like you don't know me?"

"Well, because I don't." I moved faster, hearing Erik's shouts of joy.

"Chicknas! Chicknas!" He giggled as he waddled as fast as his little legs could carry him. He chased after three zigzagging hens with feathery legs.

I laughed.

"Those are his favorite."

"They have hairy legs and poofy heads."

"It's their breed. They're fat rolls." Jesse smiled.

"Fat rolls?" I laughed. "Don't you mean Faverolles?" I used the correct pronunciation of *fav-uh-hole*. I looked up at him. The sun shone through his feathery hair, setting it into an auburn fire.

He looked at me without moving his head. "French hens." He winked. "But then again, you know lots about French, don't you?" At that very second, his eyes lowered to my lips.

My gaze widened and I couldn't help but look at his. "I-I, well, in a manner of speaking, I do." I lifted my chin and scowled at him to cover my slip up. He did not look away from my mouth, and it was as if time took a deep breath and held still for many heartbeats.

"Will you show me?" he said in a low husky voice.

"Show you?" My thoughts scattered, my heart thudded, and I felt my eyes widen. "Show you what?"

"One of your moves."

His eyes dropped to my feet and back up. This was silly, really. Why was I acting like a bumbling idiot when I'd known him all my life? Instead, I said as I walked past him to Erik, "What happened to you?"

"How do you mean?" He jogged to catch up to me.

"Well, last I remembered, you were short and f—"

"Oh!" He laughed, drawing out his *h*. "Yeah, well, it happened to both of us."

He nudged my shoulder and I lost my balance. Me! Lose my balance? Unheard of. He was faster than I and caught my waist before I could topple over an unsuspecting hen. "What did?" I prompted, whispering in a strangled voice.

I'd been handled like this before by many ballerinos. There was Ivan when he hoisted me into the air, then Rod as he touched my waist when I *pirouetted* around him. Then there was Nikoli and Adrik and—too many to count as I'd called them all my lords of leaping. But when Jesse's hands steadied my waist, I felt his body heat sear through my cotton T. I stepped back and slapped his hands away.

"I'm sorry. I didn't mean to—what did I just do?" He blinked, obvious confusion darkening his brow.

What a disaster. I turned away before he could catch my embarrassment. "Erik, show me where the chickens live."

"O' hew," Erik said in his two-year-old diction.

I ran up to him as he held his little hand up to me, which I gladly took. The chicken coop was not like anything I remembered. It was inside a huge barn I hadn't noticed before. I stared up at the rafters and tools and hay bales stacked way high. I pursed my lips and whistled.

"Yeah, Dan built this for your mom as a wedding gift."

I turned to him with a lift of my eyebrow. "Really?" Envy made my nails dig into my palm. When my parents were together, we lived like poor people.

Always scraping away to make ends meet. I supposed I had nothing to complain over since Dad landed a most coveted job as a highly-favored corporate attorney. Lucky for Julie, she followed his steps as his paid intern. Me? Ha. I preferred the arts.

"Did you know Dan built a second floor to the house?" Jesse asked, staring at the tip of his boot as he shuffled a stray piece of hay.

"I kinda figured that, but I didn't pay too much attention." Maybe Julie was right about my being so distracted? "Never mind."

Erik pulled from me and darted away. A boisterous and explosive sound of boking forced my eyes from Jesse's boots to Erik. He shrieked in laughter as he ran through a tight circle of chickens. In his hands, grain sprayed every which direction, increasing the feathered frenzy.

"Erik, I think it's time to wash up." I glanced out the entrance and saw that the shadows had moved to near invisible. Noon, already? "Time for lunch." I launched for the little boy and plunked him on my hip. He hurled the rest of the feed at the squabbling bunch and clapped his hands.

"Cora?"

The tone of nervousness in Jesse's voice snared my attention. "Yes?"

He spoke to the piece of hay at his boot. "I'd love to take you out riding during Erik's nap."

"It sounds like Mom does stuff like that all the time, but is that safe?" I looked at Erik.

"Do you see that tree there?" He pointed past the open barn doors, past the house, past the front yard. It was up a green rolling hill beside a tight grove and pond.

"The place where we'd go swimming?" I felt my eyebrows pitch into my hairline. "You aren't asking me to—?" I covered my chest protectively.

His face shown shock one second and the next, he burst out laughing. "Cora, you sure are something else." He moved toward me as if to pull me into a hug but veered off to the side with a gentle nudge. "I didn't knock you off your feet that time."

"That's because I'm holding Erik."

He turned around and walked backward. A bad habit, really. "But I intend

19

to sweep them from beneath you."

Whatever that meant.

He tipped his hat and turned back around, giving me a full view of himself without having to hide my shame.

"Uh, Jesse?"

"Yes?" He turned over his shoulder, his eyebrows high.

My stomach flipped. "You said that 'it happened to both of us' right before you pushed me." *When I slapped your hands away.* "What did you mean by that?"

"Hey." He turned completely to me, his eyes dancing. "I nudged you. You are the one who lost your feet, Miss Ballerina."

I batted the air with a dismissive wave. "Tell me."

"I only meant to say that you and I both grew up." His gaze caressed my face with meaningful depth before he whipped around and jogged back into the stables. "See you at one."

"Wait, don't you want to come in for lunch?" I gasped, realizing how forward I sounded. You'd think that New York would toughen me. In many ways it did, but being around Jesse and seeing how much he changed did things to me.

"No thank you. I have my own," he called out.

"Oh, I see how you are!" I laughed, grateful for the reprieve. "Come on, Erik. Let's go carve dinosaurs out of apples."

"Wheee! Dinosows!"

Chapter Five

horses and hospitals

fter a good washing up and pretending to be a dinosaur eating apple dinosaurs, Erik let me tuck him into his car-bed. He flipped to his side and snuggled with his favorite blankie.

"Sleep well, snuggle buggles," I said.

He waved me away.

I laughed at his dismissal. After making sure the baby monitors were on and the receiving end was fastened to my belt, I was ready to ride with Jesse. My hands shook as I smoothed my top over my hips. "Okay, Jesse, let's do this."

I did a breath check before stepping out into the sweltering heat. And there he stood. I inhaled sharply and imagined Tiana shooting his photo. Before I realized what I was doing, I whipped out my phone and captured the image of Jesse standing coolly between two restless horses, bridled and ready to go.

"What was that for?" he called, turning to Zorro, Mom's black Friesian.

"Tiana," I said in a lighthearted tone and strolled forward.

"Tiana?"

"She's a lover of photography." I hesitated when I reached Acorn. Did she really remember me?

"Ah." He must have noticed my anxiety. "I've worn out Acorn a bit for you so she plays nice."

Nervous laughter slid from my throat. "Thank you."

"You have changed a lot, Cora."

"Well, so have you," I returned but with an attitude.

"Whoa there, that's not how I meant it."

"How did you mean it, then?" I gazed at him over Acorn's saddle, wondering how I was going to mount her without falling flat on my *derrière*. Goodness.

"Well, for starters, you're much taller and powerfully built," he said.

"Oh, like your truck?" I could only imagine him owning a double cab, long bed with a lifted suspension.

"How do you know I drive a truck? I could drive a Volkswagen buggy."

"Oh, sure you do!" I flicked my eyes to him before gazing back at the saddle.

"Would you like some help there?"

"Me? Uh, no. I've done this a billion times before. I don't need anyone's help." With that, I stuck my foot high up into the stirrup and launched myself over Acorn. Too much power, I flipped over the saddle onto the other side. I didn't even have time to scream because Jesse was there, receiving me into his arms as if he knew I'd do such a thing. I stared at him with helpless rage, daring him to laugh. But he did not. Instead, he lowered his face, his gaze dropping to my mouth.

My entire body halted with unexpected longing and I caught my breath. Waiting. Waiting for the kiss that never happened. With a small huff, Jesse loosened his arms, and I slipped from his embrace.

I cleared my throat and tucked a fallen lock behind my ear. "You know."

I straightened my clothes, pretending he didn't just try to kiss me. "I can sure rock the stage." I laughed at myself. "But out here, I'm two left feet and all thumbs bundled up in one clumsy person." I shook my head, avoiding his eyes.

"Well, you know, you can't be perfect at everything." His voice was hoarse.

His tone surprised me and I couldn't help but look into his eyes. What I found there took me aback. His dark brown eyes smoldered and I forgot how to breathe. I cleared my throat again and looked away. "Acorn sure is very fuzzy." I giggled, patting her. "I guess that's what happens when it gets cold out." Though I thought Texas winters were mild didn't mean Texans felt the same.

"You've been feeling it too. Don't tell me you haven't."

"Feeling what?" I whispered. My chest fluttered like a wild, trapped bird.

He gazed sharply at my mouth. "You know."

"I do?" Cognizance finally broke through the surface of my trance, and one corner of my mouth tilted into a mischievous smile.

"Aw, Cora." He shook his head with a soft chuckle. "You should know I've always had a thing for you."

"What?" I guffawed. I blinked hard, trying to remember short and awkward Jesse in love with me. "Do you call chasing me around the coop with a toad in your hands a thing?" I laughed harder. "What about dropping grasshoppers down my shirt? And the rock in my boot?"

"Okay, you got me." He held his hands up in surrender, the little dimple in his cheek showing. "But in my defense, it was not a rock but an acorn."

"An acorn?" I laughed until my tears blurred his face.

"It was a promise acorn," his voice cracked over the word *promise*. "Don't you recall the promise acorn?"

"Ah, yes, the promise acorn." I choked. And here I thought it was just a dream that he promised to court me when we were old enough. "But we were just kids."

"Yes, and you were and have always been the most beautiful girl I've ever seen."

He spoke with such passion it had me look at him twice. When he didn't back down, I turned to Acorn's saddle and bit my lip. "Thank you."

"I mean it."

"I know," I said just as softly. The promise acorn. "Is that where Acorn got her name?" I turned to him after successfully mounting her.

"What do you think?" he asked as he glided onto Zorro's back.

His grace took my breath away. Not the kind you'd see in my dance partners, but in a graceful sort of rugged way.

"Race you?" He challenged and was off before I could answer.

"No, no!" I cried out, not wanting to start off on Acorn like that. Without permission, Acorn sprang after Zorro. Their hooves sounded like wild drumming beneath me. I screamed and clung to the reins. We tore through the yard, past the entrance, wound up the hill, and came to a sudden stop by the pond where a few swans and geese quarreled. My brain continued to spin as my life flashed before my eyes.

"Are you okay?" Jesse dismounted. He patted Zorro, led him to the water, and came to me.

"I can do this." I shook him off.

He smiled, stepped back, and watched.

"What?"

"I'm here in case you need me."

"I don't need you," I said, laughing. How wrong that sounded, but he knew what I meant. I swung my leg in a very calculating sort of swing and turned my torso toward him. When both knees faced his chest, I dared to slide off. Misjudging everything, I tumbled forward, but Jesse was there to catch me.

"Are you doing this on purpose?"

"Doing what?"

"Looking like a horse novice?" We clung together, gazing into one another's eyes.

Matchmaker haunted my thoughts and I gave him a weak smile.

"Or are you sending me a message?" he whispered.

"Don't flatter yourself," I whispered back. Did I play clumsy on purpose?

"What *did* you do to my acorn?"

I blinked at the unexpected change of topic and slowly disengaged from his arms before I lost myself. "Your acorn?" What acorn? I couldn't think straight.

"Oh, did you really forget?"

"Uh … would you be mad at me if I did?" Like I'd admit such to him, even if I did remember. I scrunched my face and glanced at him from beneath my lashes.

He laughed. "Of course not. I wouldn't trade you in for an acorn."

I laughed weakly and decided to change the subject. "It seems you have too much time on your hands to be thinking of acorns." I gave him an innocent look. "What do you do besides ride horses and chase chickens, again?"

He burst out laughing with a shake of his head.

"Milk the cows?" But I knew Mom didn't own cows.

"No, the milkmaids milk the cows." His expression turned smug. "I, on the other hand, do not chase chickens but Coras."

"Coras?" It was my turn to laugh.

His eyelids lowered into a burning smolder. "You."

Just then, the baby monitor picked up the sound of the ringing landline. The machine answered, and Dan's voice sounded rushed. "Cora, we've been trying to call your cell, but I forgot there's no service out there."

"Something's wrong," Jesse and I said at the same time, staring at the baby monitor.

"I've had to take your mother to the hospital. She's having the baby early. Please forgive the sudden change of plans as we weren't prepared for this, especially with Christmas just around the bend. Oh, and Cora? Keep Danielle and Trey in your prayers." There was a sharp click.

Trey was the baby's name. I turned to Jesse, speechless. "Mom!" I shouted, belatedly. I turned to Acorn but didn't feel confident enough to ride her back. So, I spun around and sprinted home.

"Cora!" Jesse called, but I didn't stop. Hard galloping sounded behind me and he pulled the reins sharply. For a heart-stopping moment, Zorro raised to his hind legs but landed with his rider intact. "We'll get Acorn later."

Jesse held his hand out to me and I took it without a second thought. I flew through the air and wrapped my leg around the horse's rump and clung to Jesse's muscular back. I buried my face and prayed as I've never prayed before.

Chapter Six

acorns and reality

M y stomach twisted as I lay stretched across the sofa in the living room. Jesse kept casting worried glances at me as he cooked supper. Erik played with his trucks and horses at my feet, so unaware of the heartbreaking news.

I couldn't remember the details. Something about a breech and bleeding and—I burst into a new set of tears. Oh, Mom. What was I going to do? How I prayed she and Trey would survive.

"And it's going to be Christmas!" I wailed in my tears.

"Chwistmas!" Erik sang, pointing to the huge, decorated tree. "Wights, pwease! Wights."

I covered my face and turned my back to him, unable to think.

"It's okay, I'll turn them on," I heard Jesse say.

I couldn't handle this. Not again. I sobbed. Mom nearly died having Erik.

Miraculously, they both rebounded. How could I have forgotten? "Why does this keep happening to her? What if neither survive?"

"Cora," Jesse said from close by. I felt his warmth pressing in all around as I heard him kneel beside me. "Our prayers have to work. They do." He touched my back and glided his comforting hand along my shoulder.

I nodded, soaking in his soothing stroke. "But how will we know?"

"Well, I prayed in such a way that we will."

I shifted on the couch until I faced him. "Will it work?"

He traced the pathway of my tears and dried them with his knuckles. "Hope and faith go hand in hand." He lowered his forehead to mine, his eyes closed as he clasped my hands.

I nodded, licking my chapped lips.

"Please stop crying. I don't want Erik to know."

"Erik?" I turned my head. Jesse accommodated me by acting as my counterbalance and aided me into a sitting position. Erik sat on the rug, making his dinosaur fly through the air in the bed of a little pick-up truck. "Okay." I sniffled.

"Come here." Jesse nodded, his whisper low and deep.

I angled my knees aside and scooted forward. His arms warm and comforting. His heart pounded against my ear, and his presence swallowed me. Time slowed. How safe and loved and alive this felt. Please never let this end.

"Cora?" he whispered.

I lifted my head and he combed my hair from my eyes. There was a fiery passion behind his gaze that sucked me in. "What?" My voice squeaked.

His gaze intensified and he lowered his head, his lips parting. My eyes on his mouth. My heart raced. I held still, waiting for his kiss.

"Wheeee!" Erik shrieked. "Fog! Fog!" At that very second, the smoke detectors trilled, and Jesse tore from me with a cold whoosh.

"Shoot! The pork chops."

I touched my unkissed lips and watched Jesse deal with the burnt food. A lazy smile pulled at my mouth and I sighed. Despite his effort, my heart still ached as I thought of Mom, but all I could do was pray and take care of Erik as promised. How grateful I was for Jesse's reassuring presence.

I slid to the carpet and watched Erik. He had no idea. None whatsoever. How painful it would be if Mom died; he might not even remember her. Dread stole through me. "What will happen to Erik?" But I couldn't make myself say the rest.

"Stop right there!" Jesse said in an authoritative tone from the kitchen. His expression was just as severe.

"O-okay. I will." I thinned my lips and picked up a little truck and cut a path through the fluffy rug with its wheels. "Look, Erik, a little street."

"Yay!" He grabbed a car in each hand and followed the little road I made.

After a hopeless battle with the pork chops, Jesse decided to go out into town to get pizza. I didn't dare tuck Erik into bed after his bath. We waited for Jesse's return after I fed Erik breakfast leftovers. With his little body nestled inside the circle of my arms, we dozed in front of the glowing ambiance of the lit Christmas tree.

The last thing I remembered seeing was the Nativity. Oh, how perilous Mary had it back then. No pain meds. No hospital beds. No medical equipment. No knowledge to turn babies around from inside. No heart monitors or anything of the like.

In my dream, I was Mary. A shawl draped around my head, covering part of my face to protect me from the dust and harsh sun. The donkey I sat upon was unpleasant compared to Acorn's tailored saddle. A tall man draped in robes and a head covering led my mount by a rope. I could feel every bump in the road as we traced the curve of the rudimentary path.

So many miles to travel. How did Joseph manage on foot? How did Mary? She was practically due and here she sat on a donkey to boot!

At that moment, the tall man turned to look at me, his eyes sad but smile tender and reassuring.

Jesse?

He returned his gaze to the road ahead, and I saw a glittering city dotting the horizon. Relief flooded me and I laughed with joy.

I knew what happened next.

No room. There would be no room for us to stay. How terrible! And to have the baby in a barn full of animals? Manure? Smells? My stomach turned. My throat tightened and hot tears stung my eyes.

"It's going to be okay. You'll see," my Joseph-Jesse said in a low timbre.

"How do you know?" My voice tripped over my tight throat.

"Because I believe in miracles."

So did I.

I felt his strong arms slide under my body and lift me. I curled into him, my fingers digging into his robes as he carried me deeper into the dark and stuffy barn. His hands brushed my damp hair from my face and dried my tears. His lips pressed to my forehead and lingered there as he whispered a prayer for me and the baby. A sweet feeling of peace burned through me and I smiled.

"Thank you," I whispered, lifting my lips to his. The kiss was soft and innocent.

"You need to sleep now. I'll be here if you need me."

I nodded and curled into myself. I brought the blankets up and over my shoulder, my stomach clenching with pain. My derrière was sore from riding for so long. I winced but made myself sleep. I felt the night draw later and then the cries of a baby wrenched me awake.

"What was that?" I called, blinking hard into the darkness. There were no sheep nor goats nor donkeys. No manure nor scratchy hay nor mangers. "Where am I?"

Again, the same baby wailed.

I bolted upright and crashed to the floor with a loud thump. My hand glided against smooth wooden planks and something that felt much like a shoe. "A shoe?"

"Cora, are you alright?" a man's voice sounded as steps thundered up what sounded like stairs. "I'll get Erik, stay there."

Erik? I blinked. The dimness of the hall nightlight filtered into the bedroom I was in. I shivered, thinking of my dream. It felt so real. I was Mary, Jesse was Joseph. I suppose my rump ached because of the hard ride on Acorn. As for my stomach clenching, maybe sympathy pains for Mom?

"Oh, Mom," I whispered, rolling to my back. I stared up at the ceiling and spied Julie's old glow-in-the-dark star constellations. A weak smile tugged at my lips. A cluster of brighter stars demanded my attention, and I sat up to take a closer look. No. It was a huge star the size of my palm. The only one its size. "Please"—I clasped my hands—"please let this mean something." With my heart in my mouth, I rose to my feet and steadied myself.

Jesse came into my room but without Erik.

"Where is he?" I asked, looking down in case he clung to Jesse's jeans.

"Asleep. He had a nightmare."

"Is he okay?"

"He's alright." Jesse grazed the side of my arm.

My arm responded wildly to his touch. Gooseflesh prickled and I rubbed it away.

"Cold?"

"No." I sighed. "Did you carry me to bed?" Feeling tired, I sat on the floor.

Jesse copied me. "I did. Was that okay?"

"Did you also kiss me?" I looked at his lips and blushed.

"Uh, yes?" It was his turn to blush. "It was innocent."

I covered my mouth. After several seconds, I cleared my throat and broke our gaze to look at my hands.

"I apologize. It was wrong of me. At the moment, you'd asked and I couldn't say no."

"I asked?" I raised widened eyes.

His blush deepened.

"Well." I cleared my throat. "I had this poignant dream that you—" I stopped. How would he take that? I mean, I really didn't know him, right? Wasn't it he who said that we'd grown up after all? Just how much did we grow up? I could make out his handsome face in the semidarkness. He watched me intently.

"Yes?"

"Jesse, what really brought you back here? You were off to college. I moved to New York." If he really liked me as he insisted, it made no sense that he'd move to Texas instead.

He shook his head. "You didn't move to New York." Before I could object, he said, "Your dad moved to New York."

"Same difference. My home school is there. My sister is there. My life is there."

"Your mom is here," he said as if that explained everything.

I opened my mouth but couldn't say anything to that. "True." I bowed my head in agreement.

"Acorn is here."

I nodded, a tiny smile on my lips. I loved Acorn, but I had honestly outgrown her. "But still. I was in New York. You could've moved there if you really wanted to be with me. So why here?" I felt my gaze harden a bit.

"Your heart is here."

"See, that's where I think you're w—"

"Cora, please don't." He tossed his hair with a choppy breath. "I came back after my third year in hopes to find you. I remember the day New York ripped this family apart. Your dad had an opportunity to do his work in San Antonio as well, and you cried so hard, my heart broke."

I remembered bawling and I snorted. "I was a brat, Jesse."

"No, you weren't. You've always been honest and genuine. I mean it when I say you are the most beautiful girl I've ever known."

"I hardly believe that. You're so, so—" I laughed a grating sound.

"I'm so what?" He almost sounded defensive.

"You went to school in the UK. The UK, Jesse! Did you drop out of—what was it, Oxford? Why would you leave all that for-for this?"

"I thought you knew." His voice deadpanned. "And I didn't drop out."

I rolled to my feet with a scoff. "It can hardly be the answer. I mean what I say that I was a brat. I can't believe you had fallen for me that hard. We—you—were just kids. Kids!" I looked at his beautiful face and felt like a huge heel. Why was I pushing him away?

"I graduated from high school and left for college. Yes, you are right about being just kids. But I've lived and everything fell short compared to you."

"You compared everything to me?"

"That's not exactly how I meant." He stood.

"Then what?" I became angry for some odd reason. "I doubt there is no one out there who shines brighter than me, who is more beautiful, more talented."

"That's not it."

"Then what is?" I nearly shouted.

"Why are you acting like this?" Jesse looked hurt.

"I don't understand how you could like me so much."

"It's not a matter of liking. Gosh, Cora, don't you get it?"

"No, I don't so why don't you just get it over with and tell me what it is?"

"Get it over with? Get it over with? What's that supposed to mean?" His voice broke.

"If I hurt you so much, then I don't deserve you."

"Why are you doing this? I thought we—"

"Just because we grew up together, you think that ties together your silly acorn promise? Ha!" I backed away from him, my heart shattering. *Cora, what are you doing?* "You know what, just go, Jesse." I marched over to Julie's dollhouse, dug my way through the little bedroom until I found the stupid acorn hiding under the blanket of the little bed, and threw it at Jesse. "What does it matter, you'll leave me anyway. Get out."

"Cora, please don't do this. You're under a lot of stress. You're—"

"I don't know what it is you studied out there, but you don't know me very well. You think you're in love with me. But you aren't. I am not that little girl anymore. I've shattered and broken and grew back into this crooked old tree. Please go before I throw something bigger than your acorn!"

I marched over to him and placed my hands on either of his hard pectorals and shoved him.

Jesse crashed into the wall behind him. He staggered to his feet and gave me the same look Mom had given Dad when he stormed out of the house that one night.

"I love you, Cora. Always have. Always will. And it has nothing to do with little girls or beauty or talent. Nothing. Think about that. Just call out my name if you need me. Good night, Cora."

With that, he turned on his heel and skipped down the stairs. The door slammed behind him and then he was gone. I stood there in Julie's bedroom, numb, still as a statue in shock for ten minutes at what I'd just done. I crumpled to the rug in a rage of helpless wails.

Chapter Seven

my Christmas miracle

M orning came and I awoke to the bright sun pouring around my face. I could hear the birds calling to each other just outside my window. To my surprise, I lay on the floor, my clothes creased in tight, sharp folds and my hair a mountainous mess. I clambered to my feet and stared at the clock.

2 p.m.?

"Erik!" My heart thudded and I raced into his bedroom. His bed was made, his room tidy. "Erik!" I scampered down the stairs and saw the kitchen door open. The screen was unlocked. I swore and raced out and into the hot afternoon. The horses grazed contentedly in the fields, the chickens scratched about. I scanned the pigs as they lazily wallowed in the mud. My stomach fell.

I blindly ran back into the house, my hands chilled and trembling. I guessed I didn't pay attention to where I was going because I crashed into someone.

"Cora, are you okay?"

Jesse.

Relief flooded me so hot, so fast, so powerfully, my knees gave out. Jesse swept me from my feet and carried me to the sofa. "Erik's missing." There was a tight knot in my chest.

"He's napping."

"Not in his b-bed."

"He's asleep on the couch."

I glanced across the room and found him sleeping like the sweet little angel he was. Relief, though short-lived, overcame me. I remembered Mom and cleared my throat. "How is she?"

"No news."

I dissolved into tears.

"I still believe in miracles, you know."

"Jesse, I don't deserve you. I am so mean." I tried to push him away but was too weak. He set me down and brushed my hair from my face. "Don't you hate me?"

"Why would I?"

"Because of the things I said."

"That was not you talking."

"The words came straight out of my mouth."

"That was the pain talking."

I laughed and cried at the same time.

"Just lay there while I make you breakfast."

"Jesse, it's two in the afternoon."

"And you just woke up."

"Yes."

"And you need to break your fast, right?"

"You won." I laughed a watery laugh with a shake of my head.

"Plus, I figured something out the second you hurled the acorn of death at me."

I giggled. He was so fresh and clean and so handsome. An ache tore through my middle. How could he love me?

"I asked myself, if Cora didn't so much care for me as she so claims, then why did she keep my acorn promise all these many years?"

"Because I forgot about it?"

"But you remembered. You even kept it with you."

"I live in New York."

"It doesn't matter where you are in this world, you still kept it." Something dinged and a knowing smile curved his lips. "Be right back." He hurried into the kitchen, leaving me to contemplate the universe.

"You never give up, do you?" I asked, watching him.

"I'm still here, aren't I?" He carried a baking dish with oven mitts.

I laughed. "Yes, you are. About last night." My breath caught as I thought of how horrible I was to him. "I am so very sorry. I didn't know—"

He was suddenly in front of me. "Shh. You don't need to apologize. I completely understand."

I dove into the chocolate warmth of his eyes. "I'm still sorry."

"I do have something else for you, though." His eyes shined.

"What do you have for me?" I couldn't resist.

"It's supposed to snow. As in, a whole lot."

"Whatever." I rolled my eyes, thinking about the hot humidity.

"It happens."

"Not here in Texas."

"It has happened."

"It'll be a miracle."

His face grew serious, his eyes intensified. "I believe in miracles. Don't you believe in miracles, Cora?"

"It's possible."

So, we spent the rest of the day preparing for a big storm. I didn't tell Erik because I believed it wouldn't happen, but we had the blankets folded and the wood chopped beside the hearth. Jesse went as far as setting out the hot-chocolate-and-marshmallow ingredients along the countertop.

"Thnow?" Erik asked, looking at the goodies with excitement as we made a gingerbread house.

"Did you tell him?" My eyes narrowed.

"Me? I'd never upstage you."

I arched an eyebrow, knowing how it felt to be upstaged by a prima donna. AKA, Yana.

The closer the night drew, the closer to insanity I became. Dan still hadn't called. The snow hadn't fallen, and it was still hotter than Jesse's breakfast casserole; recipe courtesy of his grandma. I found myself sitting on the porch swing with Erik on my lap. We watched the stars blink on with the porch light off.

Jesse joined us, phone in hand. Just in case.

"Tomorrow's Christmas, you know." I could hardly talk. I was so drained of emotion as well as stamina and strength. So much for being a powerful ballerina.

"I know," Jesse whispered, reaching across to brush Erik's hair from his eyes.

"What're we going to do?"

"Let it come."

I huffed. Wise answer. What else could we do? Before we knew it, dark clouds gathered in the East. The wind began to howl and with it, warm rain. We ran inside, waking Erik into excitement. We watched movie after Christmas movie until he could no longer keep his eyes open. Before he went off to bed, he muttered, "thnow?"

"I promise to let you know as soon as it does," I said, feeling like a lousy liar. Driving rainstorms were nothing new here. I could hear the rain pounding against the porch and window panes.

"Okay," he said in his little voice.

I carried him to bed, tucked him in, and kissed his head. I made it down to the living room, Jesse had turned the television off and sat there by the glow of the Christmas tree.

"Where have you been staying?" I finally asked him. He said all I had to do was call out his name. "I mean, how did you know?" I pointed up the stairs at Erik.

He raised the baby monitor and shook it along with the wiggling of his eyebrows. "Just say my name."

"You've been listening in?"

"Yep."

My face grew hot. I thought back on anything incriminating I could have said. "And?"

"And, what?"

Not wanting him to know what I was thinking, I said instead, "Did I tell you I had a dream of you?"

"You were about to."

"You were Joseph and I was Mary." His bright and innocent gaze turned deep and hot. It was such a swift turn-around that I lost my train of thought.

"And?" he prompted.

"And, I, uh. I can't continue with you looking at me like that." I turned away.

"How am I looking at you like?" he said in a velvety tone.

"Like the house will catch fire without a match."

"Really?"

"I thought I was having a baby, and I remember every painful detail of riding the donkey as you led it into Bethlehem." I slowed at the last part, remembering quite vividly the glittering city on the horizon. "It felt so real, I could almost touch it."

"That's how I feel about you."

"What? That I'm so real you could almost touch me?" I felt too embarrassed to meet his gaze.

"Don't look away from me. There's no shame in it but that's not how I mean."

"There're lots of things you don't mean."

"That's why we talk it out."

"Mm-hm." Now I felt like the village idiot.

"Don't do that to yourself." He rose from the sofa and knelt in front of me. He took the red licorice from my hand and put it on the plate with the rest of the gingerbread house makings. It was nearly done anyway. "Don't doubt yourself. You're smarter than you think. I meant that what I feel for you, what I think you feel for me is so real, I can feel it. I can touch it." He pressed his hands to his heart, his voice intense.

"You never did say what it was about me you liked," I said breathlessly. I was in awe at his tenacity. I'd never had anyone feel this way about me. It was always just talk for something in return.

"Your compassion. Your kindness and forgiving nature. You put others before you."

I shook my head. "Childish things of the past."

"But you came here instead of performing for your Nutcracker." He reached out for my hand and stroked my knuckles with his thumb. I closed my eyes, enjoying the sensation.

"I had no choice," I whispered.

"Yes, you did."

I disagreed.

"You had every reason to back out. School. Your ballet. Distance. Weather. Julie. Your dad."

"Those are not factors at all. Where are you getting this from?"

"Your mom."

"No." I pulled from him, but he didn't let go.

"It was your mom who told me how strongly you felt about her losing Erik. Julie is still bitter about the remarriage. Your dad is engaged."

"He what?"

Jesse shook his head. "Don't you remember how your dad came to you, asking you if you want to be around when your mom has Trey?"

I was about to shake my head when a subtle memory pierced me. It was of Dad talking to me as we discussed my role in The Nutcracker. He had asked if I would rather be with Mom while she gave birth over Christmas break than at his engagement party. I blinked from the vivid images of the conversation.

"How do you know?"

Jesse's head lowered, but he glimpsed at me through his long lashes. "Your mom told me."

"I had forgotten that. Why?" It was so unlike me to forget such detail.

"Maybe your mind forgets things like that on purpose and only remembers the big and safe things you're used to."

"But that's silly. It's such an important element. I don't believe you."

"It's all about loss and pain. You've suffered so much already from your parents."

I closed my eyes. I'd never known that about myself. Just how many other things did my mind erase just to protect myself? "Why-why is Mom so fascinated with you?"

"Because of how I feel about you."

Matchmaker. Mom's words came back to me. I laughed a light breathy sound. It was so soft I barely heard it myself. "How did she know that I would, uh, like you back?" Was *like* really the word I was looking for? I knew I felt more than *like* for him.

A little smile curved his lips. "The acorn."

"No." I laughed. "No. I can't believe it. I don't believe it."

"Your mom told me how much you raved about it. She told me you had made a little shrine around it in Julie's dollhouse and then how you told all your friends."

Strange, but I couldn't remember that at all. "Sounds made up."

"It goes back to your heart shutting out all good things and holding onto the things that feel the safest."

"I don't know if I can believe that." I squirmed, feeling uncomfortable.

"I want to see you dance. Will you show me?"

"Here? Now?" I balked. I looked at my clothes. "But I'm not dressed for it." Jeans were far from dancing material.

"I bet you have leggings or something of the sort up there."

"You're serious?"

"Yes." He looked hurt.

"Okay. Sure." I stood and his face lit up. "On one condition." I just had to have the last laugh.

"Anything for you."

"I want you to tip your cowboy hat and say 'yes ma'am' to me."

"What?" His eyes widened as well as his smile.

"You heard me!" I called over my shoulder as I pranced up the stairs. What a sick city girl fantasy. Just thinking of him doing that made me super giddy. I decided to go all out for him. I'd be a liar if I said I didn't bring my ballet stuff with me. I bought the whole thing; I owned the costuming to The Nutcracker's leading role, Clara.

Thirty minutes later, I backed from the mirror. How glad I was for tight ballerina buns to keep the frizz tamed.

My heart sank as I thought of Mom. I dropped to my knees and prayed hard. I prayed for Mom's stamina and strength and for the survival of both mother and baby. My thoughts reverted to Mary and her little baby Jesus. I thought of Joseph's love as well as his valor.

"Faith, Cora, faith." I reprimanded myself when I was done.

With a bow, I flitted down the stairs to where Jesse sat on the sofa with his head in his hands.

"Are you okay?" I asked, dropping down to one knee.

He gave a start. "I didn't hear you."

"What's wrong?"

He smiled, but it didn't touch his eyes. "You're so very beautiful." It was as if his eyes devoured me. They traveled everywhere across my face and eventually dropped down the length of me and then back to my eyes. It was a painfully slow process, but I took pleasure in the glow of his basking. "Inside and out."

"Well." I rose to my feet. "Here I am." I looked around the living room, but with our gingerbread project and presents about, I couldn't dance.

"Maybe it was a bad idea after all." He stood. He barely glanced at me as if timid.

"What about outside?"

"But it's awful. The rain?"

I moved to the window, shivering at the fact that he watched my every move. I lifted the curtain aside and saw that the rain and wind had stopped. The clouds hung overhead. Heavy, white, and silent. White clouds at such a late hour?

"It's dark out," he said.

"The driveway is well lit if we flip the switch and it's smooth enough for me," I said.

We both looked at my feet and he sighed, his eyes filled with wonder. I flushed. Had I mentioned that he was the only person who has ever made me feel beautiful? No? Well, I guess I had forgotten because this sensation felt so divine, and now I remembered how he made me feel—even way back.

"Come on!" I grabbed his hands and walked backward. "It's my turn to walk backwards." I lifted to my toes as I moved in *pas de couru*, or small, mincing steps en pointe. His eyes shined as he watched me, and I gracefully bowed my head. As soon as we reached the garage door and turned the lights on, we darted into the night.

Once outside, I threw myself into my routine. I was clumsy because I had not stretched, but my muscles remembered the pattern. The flowing gentleness of movement. I softened my breath and my eyes and kept Jesse as my spot. I imagined the beautiful notes of the orchestra and moved along with its fluidic flow. I forced myself onward until I trembled and shined with perspiration. The contrast of air and exuding heat from my body tingled along my skin, and I shivered.

A tiny soft glow of flutter drifted past my lashes. Thinking it as my imagination, I continued with my last set of movements until, soon, my stage was filled with soft, fluttering flakes of whiteness. I ended my dance with the *grande reverence*—the most graceful bow I could offer.

At first, nothing. I didn't hear a thing. I couldn't even hear myself breathing. I looked up him and realized that it was snowing! White, heavy flakes that fell as softly as a cat on silent feet.

Jesse stood, his face as if in agony. Then, he clapped hard, slowly lifting his hands higher and higher until they reached over his bowed head. He finally hooted and hurled his hat into the air.

"Magnificent," he whispered, tears running down his face. "My dancing lady."

"Thank you." I could hardly speak as well.

"This could be the very thing we asked for." He pointed to the falling snow, his finger skyward.

"Snow?"

"The miracle." He swallowed hard, his Adam's apple dropping with the motion.

I thought of Mom. "I'm cold."

"Let's go inside before you get sick." He didn't take his eyes off me as we strolled back into the house. He flipped the driveway light off.

"Should we wake Erik? He'd love the snow," I said over a tight throat as I sat in my full ensemble on the sofa.

"Hold on a second." He replaced the hat to his head, still standing, and rolled his shoulders. I watched in awe the play of hard muscle beneath his clothes. When he was done warming up, as to what I couldn't imagine, he tilted his head to the side, raised his right hand, tipped his hat and said in the most toe-curling southern drawl I'd ever heard, "Yes, ma'am."

A delicious shiver wracked over me. I laced my hands at my chin but couldn't giggle. "Thank you," I said, too choked up for the words to come out properly.

Just then, the phone rang and I jumped. He sauntered over to answer but handed the phone to me instead. When I saw Dan calling, I lost my strength and fell back against the sofa.

"Hello, Jesse speaking?" he answered in his southern drawl. Either for my benefit or he'd forgotten he had one. He looked at me, his eyebrows rising empathetically.

I didn't want to hear it. I covered my ears and squeezed my eyes shut. No. No. This couldn't be happening. Please. I prayed so hard that I thought my heart might burst. I will be a good sister. I will stay with Erik. I will give up my life as a ballerina so that I can help Dan with the ranch. I will take Mom's place and show her just how much I do love her and her life in Texas as well as Erik and Dan. Then there was Trey…

Please forgive me, Mama, for not being a better daughter. Please.

I heard Jesse's pleading voice. His hands were gentle as they forced mine from clutching my ears. "Cora." He'd been crying. "It's your mom."

"No!" I became weak, but he pulled me to him.

"Listen, darlin'—"

"What will I tell Erik? He's only two. Please. Oh, I can't bear this. I can't."
The place where my heart was felt dark and empty and deep. How it hurt.
Oh, so much. I couldn't stop shaking.

"Cora, listen to me." Jesse tried again. "Trey was saved. Your mom? Well,
she survived the ordeal."

That was all I could hear and I dissolved into more tears. She lived?

"… will stay longer … to watch her…. She's strong."

Bringing him with me, I jumped to my feet and clutched him to me.
Feeling my resolve firming, I said through chattering teeth as I thought of
Erik in the snow, "We have to do this." I was chilled to the bone with trauma,
but I didn't care.

"But you're not feeling well."

"Jesse. For me. Please." I led him up the stairs and into Erik's room. I
bundled him with a soft, thick blanket like a newborn, and Jesse picked him
up for me. Silently, we three made our way through the house and into the
great outdoors where the snow gathered in soft, white blankets of sparkling
wonder.

"Thnow?" Erik said, bleary-eyed.

"Yes, little one, thnow," I said, feeling overjoyed as my eyes stung with
tears.

Jesse tightened his hold around me and Erik. "Now is the time to ask."

The quiver in his voice didn't get past me.

"Cora, will you be my wife?"

"Wife?" I looked at him in surprise.

"The acorn of promise, remember? Courting?"

I stared at him, confused. Maybe because I had expected Mom to die. I
still felt confused and lost. "Courting? But I'm not old enough."

"Not old enough?" Genuine confusion clouded his features. "You're
twenty-one." He blinked. "Of course, you are."

"What?" I could not, of course, step back from him because we jointly
held Erik who held his mouth open to taste the fat falling flakes of snow. I
shook my head. "Last I checked, I was seventeen."

"You were seventeen four years ago, yes. Cora, if it's too sudden, I'm more than pleased to court you until you're ready."

"I-I don't know what to say. I…" I closed my eyes and breathed. Was I not seventeen when I left New York? I tried to remember, but my brain refused to cooperate. Maybe it was one of those mind-stopping things Jesse had explained to me where I block everything good and fill it with bad to protect myself from disappointment. He'd listed some things about me. Didn't he say school? Ballet? Julie? Dad? I thought harder. I suddenly remembered Tiana turning twenty-one earlier this year. How could I have forgotten? A breath shot out of my mouth, and I lifted wide eyes to him. A pair of doves flitted overhead as a sort of confirmation.

"I've already danced in The Nutcracker. This will be my second year running," I finally whispered, in shock. Yana was angry that I had the lead role last year and she fought me hard for it this year. Was that why I was okay to leave for Texas? Because deep down, I knew it didn't matter?

"Let go of the hurtful past and start living in the present. It's okay to enjoy all the good things in your life, to let those harmful moments die, only then can you truly live." Jesse pressed his warm lips to my jawline. "How I've always loved you."

It was as if he saved every emotion for this as the fire burned from his gaze right down to his potent touches, leaving a shivery wake of goosebumps. I lost my breath and stared at his lips as he bent his head, his dark eyelashes fluttering shut. He paused, waiting, maybe to see if I would accept him.

My body reacted fiercely to his silent proffer. I didn't hesitate. I gripped the hair at the nape of his neck with my free hand, slightly knocking his Stetson hat askew, and kissed him deeply. How soft and warm and demanding his kiss became! My worries fell away and my world righted itself. I felt my memories align themselves and I remembered just how much I cared for Jesse. I always had. Radiating warmth tingled all the way down to my toes. His arm tightened around my shoulder and he pulled me against him. With Erik in tow, he lifted me off my feet.

"And I've loved you for all my life," I said against his mouth, out of breath. "Let Yana have The Nutcracker." I looked at Jesse. "After all, I have the real thing."

The End

Author's Note

Depersonalization Disorder is a mental illness where a person removes him or herself from emotions, actions, sensations, or thoughts due to a stressful or traumatic event. In Cora's case, I exaggerated her disorder (for the sake of plot) to the point that she removed herself from the things she once cared for—her stepbrother, her mom, The Nutcracker, her age, Jesse—all stemming from her parents' divorce. Of course it doesn't help that she suffers from abandonment issues, either. Sometimes it's easier to stick with what's familiar even if it's abusive so we won't have to step out of our comfort zones and risk rejection all over again.

It takes courage to step forward and admit when something is holding you back, and even more faith to change it.

Thank you for suspending believability for the sake of experiencing Cora's growth in so short a book!

Acknowledgments

First, I'd like to thank my Father in Heaven, who has always been my Muse in all things. I owe my all to Him.

I appreciate how patient my kids, Cheyanna, Levi, Autumn, Dallas, and Weston have been while I obsess with writing, editing, formatting, illustrating, and more illustrating and more writing and even more editing. Then there's writer's blocks and soundboarding and learning curves and brainstorming—oh my! I couldn't live my dreams without their undying support.

Without Mike, my husband, I would be an insane ball of fluff, so thank you, hubby for believing in me!

I'd also like to thank Levi for allowing me to pick his handsome brain—he sure has the fiery heart of a writer. You rock! Thanks to Autumn for her undying hopeless romantic viewpoint. To Cheyanna for her blunt honesty.

Thanks to Amey Zeigler, Julie Mayerson Brown, Levi Mueller, Deb W. Kincheloe, and Autumn Mueller for your heart, eyes, brains, and smarts in helping me to get this book out.

Thanks to you, my dear readers, for being brave enough to pick this little story up and reading it to its very end. If you love this story, please post a public review—you're the best!

By the way, I've woven the Twelve Days of Christmas into the story in one form or another. Find all twelve, email them to me, and I'll email you a *Cora and Jesse Twelve Days of Christmas* seek-and-find coloring page. Have fun!

About the Author

Photo by Levi Mueller

Award-winning author Elizabeth Mueller lives in Texas with her
husband, five lively children, five indoor kitties, a few outdoor kitties, and a
whole lot of tumbleweeds. While she enjoys homeschooling the kidlets, she
thrives as a full-time writer of any genre that captures her heart.
Say hi! elizabeth.mueller.author@gmail.com
www.facebook.com/ElizabethMueller Author or visit her
website www.elizabethmueller.com

Made in the USA
Middletown, DE
13 April 2023

28651586R00035